Dear Parents and Educators,

Welcome to Penguin Young Readers! As parents and educators, you know that each child develops at his or her own pace—in terms of speech, critical thinking, and, of course, reading. Penguin Young Readers recognizes this fact. As a result, each Penguin Young Readers book is assigned a traditional easy-to-read level (1–4) as well as a Guided Reading Level (A–P). Both of these systems will help you choose the right book for your child. Please refer to the back of each book for specific leveling information. Penguin Young Readers features esteemed authors and illustrators, stories about favorite characters, fascinating nonfiction, and more!

| Skylanders Universe™ Spyro and the Giants | LEVEL **3** GUIDED READING LEVEL **M** |

This book is perfect for a **Transitional Reader** who:
- can read multisyllable and compound words;
- can read words with prefixes and suffixes;
- is able to identify story elements (beginning, middle, end, plot, setting, characters, problem, solution); and
- can understand different points of view.

Here are some **activities** you can do during and after reading this book:
- Comprehension: After reading the book, answer the following questions:
  - How many Elements are there? Describe two Elements and what powers they give the Skylanders.
  - Why did Master Eon summon Spyro?
  - Who are the Giants, and how do they help Spyro?
  - Of what Element is Tree Rex, and what are his powers?
  - How is Kaos defeated?
- Creative Writing: Master Eon has summoned you to tell you that the Skylanders need your help. What trouble are the Skylanders in now? How will you help them? Write a paragraph describing why Master Eon has called you and how you are going to respond.

Remember, sharing the love of reading with a child is the best gift you can give!

—Bonnie Bader, EdM
  Penguin Young Readers program

*Penguin Young Readers are leveled by independent reviewers applying the standards developed by Irene Fountas and Gay Su Pinnell in *Matching Books to Readers: Using Leveled Books in Guided Reading*, Heinemann, 1999.

PENGUIN YOUNG READERS
Published by the Penguin Group
Penguin Group (USA) Inc., 375 Hudson Street, New York, New York 10014, USA

USA | Canada | UK | Ireland | Australia | New Zealand | India | South Africa | China
Penguin Books Ltd, Registered Offices: 80 Strand, London WC2R 0RL, England

For more information about the Penguin Group visit penguin.com

ISBN 978-0-448-46491-6   10 9 8 7 6 5 4 3 2 1

PENGUIN YOUNG READERS

LEVEL

TRANSITIONAL
READER

3

SPYRO AND THE GIANTS

illustrated by Caravan Studio

Penguin Young Readers
An Imprint of Penguin Group (USA) Inc.

Glossary

Elements are what give the Skylanders their powers. There are eight elements: Magic, Earth, Water, Fire, Tech, Undead, Life, and Air.

Giants are the original Skylanders. They were sent away from Skylands a long time ago, but were brought back to help defeat Kaos.

Gill Grunt is a Skylander of the Water Element. He is one of Spyro's closet friends.

Kaos is an evil Portal Master. His goal is to defeat the Skylanders and take over Skylands.

Master Eon is known as the greatest Portal Master ever. He exists only in spirit form, but is still able to guide Spyro and the other Skylanders.

Portal Masters are the wisest and most powerful beings in Skylands.

Skylanders are heroes who use their Elemental powers to protect Skylands.

Skylands is a magical world made up of many floating islands. It's where the Skylanders live.

Spyro is a fiery little dragon. He is one of the leaders of the Skylanders. His Element is Magic.

"Why have you summoned me?"
Spyro asked the old Portal Master.

Master Eon had a serious
expression on his face. "Your friends
are in trouble and they need your
help," the Portal Master replied.

"The other Skylanders have been caught outside Kaos's castle. You must hurry if you are to help them," Master Eon added.

"Do you think I'll be able to save them on my own?" Spyro asked the Portal Master.

"I've called upon the Giants to aid you," Master Eon replied.

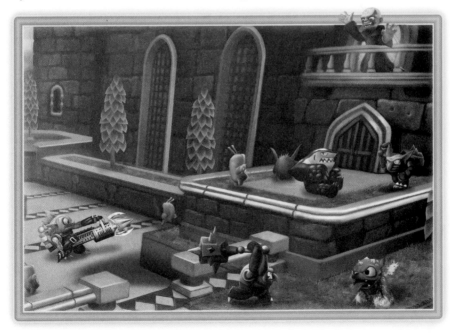

Long before Spyro's time, the Giants were responsible for protecting Skylands. They were the very first Skylanders.

Then one day, the Giants vanished from Skylands and never returned. Eventually people forgot about them. Some believed that they were only a myth and never really existed.

The Portal Masters never forgot
about the Giants and searched for a
way to bring them back. They called

the Giants to Skylands to help with
the war against Kaos.

The Giants joined the battle
alongside the other Skylanders.

11

"Giants get me all fired up!"
Spyro exclaimed. Even though
he was much smaller, he enjoyed
battling alongside the Giants. Spyro
especially liked Ninjini, the ninja
genie, because they were both of the
Magic Element.

The little purple dragon left
Master Eon and headed off across
the rocky landscape of Skylands to
Kaos's castle. As one of the leaders of
the Skylanders, Spyro felt that it was
his duty to protect his friends.

On the other side of Skylands, Tree Rex led the Giants on their way to Kaos's castle.

"We should be there shortly," he shouted. "I swear by my bark that I'll make Kaos pay."

Tree Rex was of the Life Element, which meant that it was his duty to protect the natural order of the universe. Skylanders of this Element use their abilities to create living things such as plants. Tree Rex also could use his giant wooden arm to smash anything that got in his way.

"Let's hurry up and get there,"
Crusher said to the others. "Our
friends need our help." Crusher
was a rock creature of the Earth
Element. He liked to use his giant
rock hammer to smash the earth to
defeat his enemies.

"Yeah, let's roll on out," Bouncer the Tech Giant said as he sped past the other Giants.

The Giants had to move fast if they were going to get to Kaos's castle and help save the others.

By the time Spyro had arrived at
Kaos's castle, the other Skylanders
were about to be defeated.

"My fins sure are happy to see

you," Spyro's friend Gill Grunt called
out to him. The small blue-green
fishlike Skylander had his hands full
fighting off a group of Blaster Trolls.

"You want some of this?" Spyro growled as he charged horns-first into the Blaster Trolls.

Gill Grunt and the other Skylanders cheered as Kaos's soldiers were pushed back.

But they cheered too soon. A
swarm of Trolls and other bad guys
surrounded Spyro and the other
Skylanders.

Kaos laughed. "Well, well, well,
Skylanders. It looks like I will finally
defeat you," he yelled down from the
safety of his balcony.

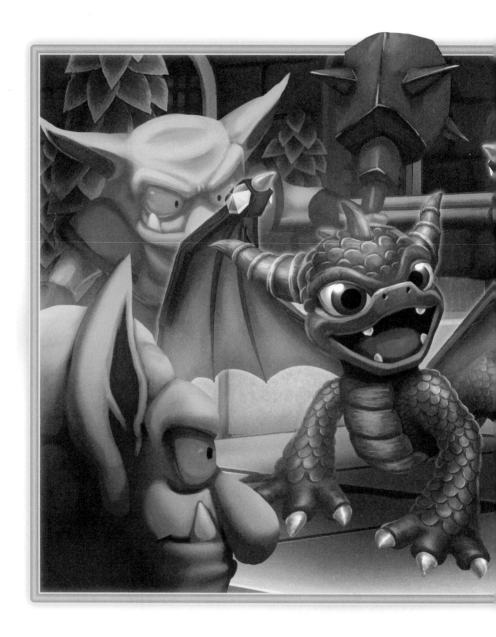

"Let's see you try," Spyro replied.
He inhaled deeply, preparing a
mighty breath of fire.

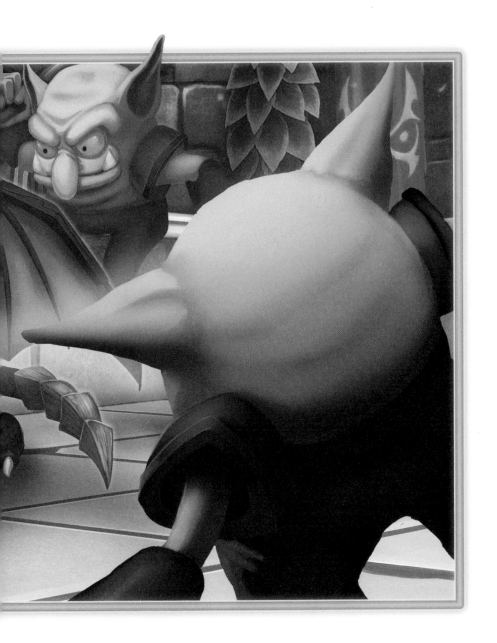

Before he could exhale, a group of
Trolls tackled Spyro to the ground.
The Skylanders were outnumbered.

A shadow fell over Kaos as he prepared for victory. As the ground started shaking, he knew what was coming. Giants.

"Don't think you'll win so easily," Tree Rex called out. "Unlike you, I'm all bark *and* all bite!"

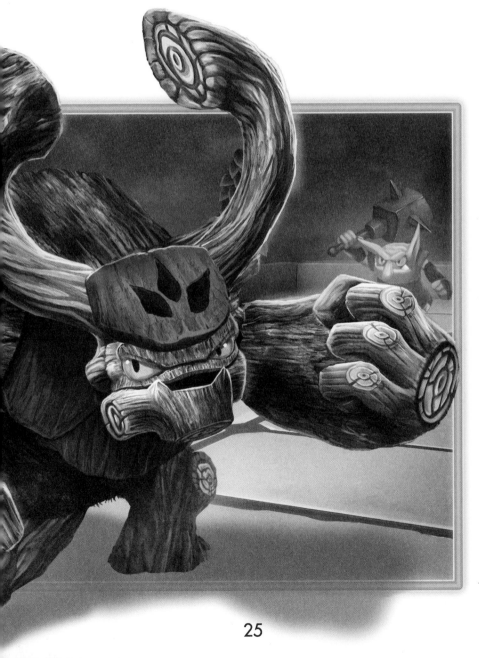

"It's *crush* hour!" Crusher said as
he raised his hammer into the air
and smashed it to the ground.

The Giant wasp named Swarm
flew past Crusher. His sharp stinger
was ready for battle.

A burst of fire rained down on a group of Trolls. Spyro looked and saw Hot Head the Fire Giant charging into the fight.

Behind him were the Giant whale Thumpback and the Undead Giant Eye-Brawl. Spyro was most excited to see Ninjini, who was of the Magic Element, just like him.

"You want some of this?" Spyro
called out to Kaos as the Giants
moved in around him.

At the sight of the Giants
approaching, Kaos fled back inside
his castle. He knew he was defeated.

Spyro and the Giants chased away the remains of Kaos's army.

They may not have been able to capture Kaos, but they were able to help their friends.

Together, the Skylanders would be there to defend all of Skylands.